SOUTH SHORE
WEBSTER

WITHDRAWN

WITHDRAWN

Emma's New Pony

A Random House PICTUREBACK®

Emma's New Pony

Story by Amy Ehrlich
Photographs by Richard Brown

SOUTH SHORE
HERBSTER

89-556

RANDOM HOUSE 🏠 NEW YORK

Text copyright © 1988 by Amy Ehrlich. Photographs copyright © 1988 by Richard Brown. All rights reserved under
International and Pan-American Copyright Conventions. Published in the United States by Random House, Inc., New York, and
simultaneously in Canada by Random House of Canada Limited, Toronto.

Library of Congress Cataloging-in-Publication Data: Ehrlich, Amy, 1942–.   Emma's new pony. (A Random House pictureback)
SUMMARY: A little girl learns to take care of her new filly. [1. Ponies—Fiction] I. Brown, Richard, ill. II. Title.
PZ7.E328Em   1988   [E]   88–1978   ISBN: 0-394-89210-0 (trade); 0-394-99210-5 (lib. bdg.)

Manufactured in the United States of America   1 2 3 4 5 6 7 8 9 0

My name's Emma and this is our pony, April. Soon April's going to have a baby. I can hardly wait!

We have lots of other horses on our farm, but April and I are special friends. My parents promised that when April's baby is born, it can be my very own pony.

My father and I work hard to get April's stall ready. She'll need lots of fresh, clean straw on the floor. It's cool and quiet in the barn. I think April likes that.

Even though she's a gray Welsh pony, my parents say April's baby will probably be black. Most gray ponies are black when they are born. April has had three other babies. She's an experienced mother and seems to be very calm about everything. She just eats and waits.

April surprises us! One morning when I run outside, the new pony is waiting. As I watch, she wobbles to her feet and stands up. She wants to be right next to her mother.

At first April won't let me touch the baby. She neighs each time I come close. I guess I'll have to wait.

But on a farm, there's always plenty to do. Besides our own horses, we keep and train other people's horses for them. Right now in our barn, we have fourteen horses in all.

Every day I help with the chores. I sweep the aisle in the barn and fill the water buckets.

That takes about half an hour. When I'm through, I go into all the stalls and say good morning to the horses.

Today I decide to clean one of the saddles. It will be a while before I can ride April again, but I want to be ready.

I use a leather soap to wash the saddle. I wash all the straps, and underneath them, too.

When the saddle is clean and dry, I polish it until it shines.

One day when April and the new pony are in the pasture, I make myself sit very still. My mom feeds April some grain and after a while, April forgets I'm there. But the baby is curious. Her ears prick up, and she comes over to see me. She is so soft and pretty, and she isn't frightened at all.

"I'm going to name you Little Flower," I tell her. Flower and I are exactly the same size.

The June days are long and
sunny. The grownups are busy
cutting hay and loading it into
the barn for our horses to eat
in the winter. There isn't much
work for me, but that's okay. I
love to sit on the pasture fence
and watch the horses. April
and Flower usually stay off by
themselves.

Flower has so much to learn!
Whatever her mother does, she
tries to imitate.

But Flower isn't the only baby on our farm. One afternoon when my father and I are taking a walk, we discover that one of our geese has had goslings.

I take a gosling over to show Flower. She is very curious.

It's time for Flower to learn about being led. My mother buckles a leather halter around her head. I talk to Flower gently the whole time and tell her there's nothing to be scared of.

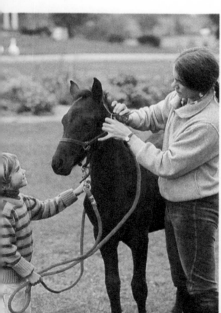

My mother leads April and I follow with Flower. I hold the
lead rope the way my parents have shown me. Flower is very well
behaved. "Good, Flower," I tell her as we walk.

I'm going to begin riding April again. My father helps me
saddle up and get ready. But there's a problem we haven't
counted on—Flower's curiosity.

My father says that a pony's curiosity helps her to learn. "Flower just wants to see what we're doing," he tells me. "She doesn't want to be left out."

89-556   SOUTH SHORE
HERBSTER

Flower seems a little ticklish. Then she discovers how good it feels. Horses and ponies need to be brushed often to keep their coats shiny.

But I think the best part of a brushing is just being close.

After the ride, we walk the horses to cool them down. Then we give them a good brushing.

As soon as Flower sees me brushing April, she wants to be brushed too.

I let her sniff the brush to get her used to it. I begin at her head and work back.

As Flower grows, she gets stronger and stronger. One day while we are having lunch, she pushes through the fence and begins eating our herb garden. "Oh, no!" cries my mother. She grabs a broom on her way outside and uses it to chase Flower away.

That afternoon my father and I tighten all the fences around the pasture.

Every two months the blacksmith comes. He trims the horses' feet and puts shoes on the riding horses.

Flower won't get shoes until she's three, but the blacksmith checks her feet anyway.

He wants to make friends with Flower so that she'll trust him later on.

"She's a nice pony," he tells us. "Why don't you enter her in the county fair?"

I think that's a great idea and so does my mother.

The blacksmith makes sure that the horseshoes are the right size for our horses. It'll be a while before this one fits Flower.

Finally! Today is the day of the county fair. We're going to take April and Flower. There's a lot to do to get ready.

Both horses must be washed and brushed. Then we braid and tie their manes with ribbons.

But the hardest part is getting them into our horse trailer. Flower won't go until April is in.

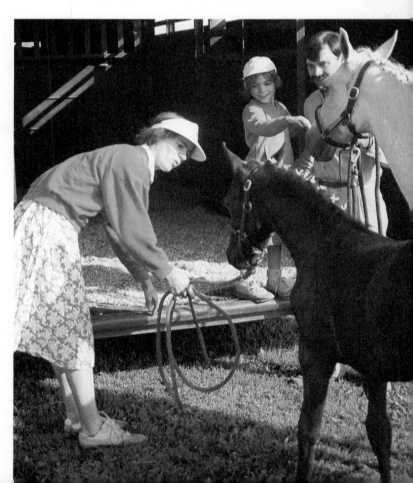

At the fair we unload the horses and groom them again.

This is the first time Flower has ever been away from home. I was worried that the noise and strange horses might make her nervous. But I stay with her and talk to her, and soon she's calm.

We walk over to the ring and they give me a number.

Our event is called the open foal class. It's for ponies up to two years old.

Flower will be judged on both appearance and manners. Right before it's our turn to go before the judges, I tell Flower to remember her training.

I'm really excited! Even though I've been to lots of
fairs and horse shows, I've never been in one before. My
mother helps us get started and then I lead Flower by myself.

Flower wins a blue ribbon. That's first place in the open foal class! I'm going to put the ribbon on her stall so that everyone can see it.

To me Flower will always be the best. She's my very own
wonderful pony.

SOUTH SHORE
WEBSTER